MOON WALK

by Dana Meachen Rau

Illustrated by Thomas Buchs

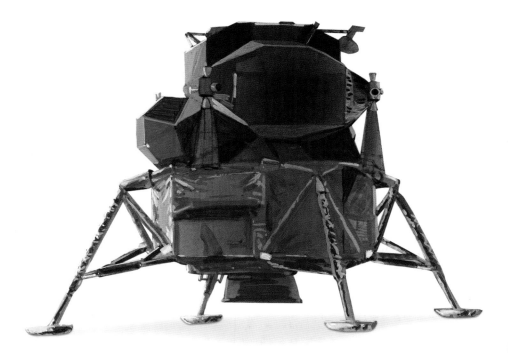

Little®
Soundprints

To Mom and Dad, for teaching me that imagination is the best entertainment — D.M.R.

To Bryan and Barry — T.B.

Published by Soundprints Division of Trudy Corporation, Norwalk, Connecticut.

Book design: Marcin D. Pilchowski
Editor: Laura Gates Galvin
Editorial assistance: Chelsea Shriver

First Edition 2003
10 9 8 7 6 5 4 3 2 1
Printed in China

Acknowledgments:
        Soundprints would like to thank Ellen Nanney and Robyn Bissette at the Smithsonian Institution's Office of Product Development and Licensing for their help in the creation of this book.

Library of Congress Cataloging-in-Publication Data is
on file with the publisher and the Library of Congress.

Table of Contents

A note to the reader:
Throughout this story you will see words in **bold letters**. There is more information about these words in the glossary. The glossary is in the back of the book.

Chapter 1

Where to Go, What to See

Tomas, Lucy, Kevin and Emma have been looking at the museum map for ten minutes, trying to decide what exhibit they should see first.

The four of them have been best friends since first grade. They do everything together—play soccer, go to the movies and go on field trips to museums. They are lucky to live in Washington, DC, near the Smithsonian Institution. There are exciting things to see everywhere!

"Okay, let's go to the **planetarium** now," Emma says as she folds the map.

"But we'll never have time to see the moon rock!" Tomas complains.

Tomas has been waiting all week to visit the National Air and Space Museum. Now he is finally here and he hasn't seen anything yet!

Tomas looks at his watch. Time is ticking away.

"I think I'll go see the moon rock now. You guys can catch up to me later," Tomas tells the group, as he walks away.

Tomas reaches a sign that reads: ACTUAL APOLLO LUNAR MODULE. "Awesome! This is just like the one that brought the first men to the moon!" Tomas says to himself.

"Wait, Tomas! Let's stick together," cries Emma as she and the others enter the exhibit.

But Tomas doesn't hear Emma, or anyone else. He is thinking about how great it must have been to be the first man on the moon.

Tomas feels a tap on his shoulder. "Neil, Neil!"

Tomas wonders who is calling him Neil. He looks around and realizes that he is no longer in the museum!

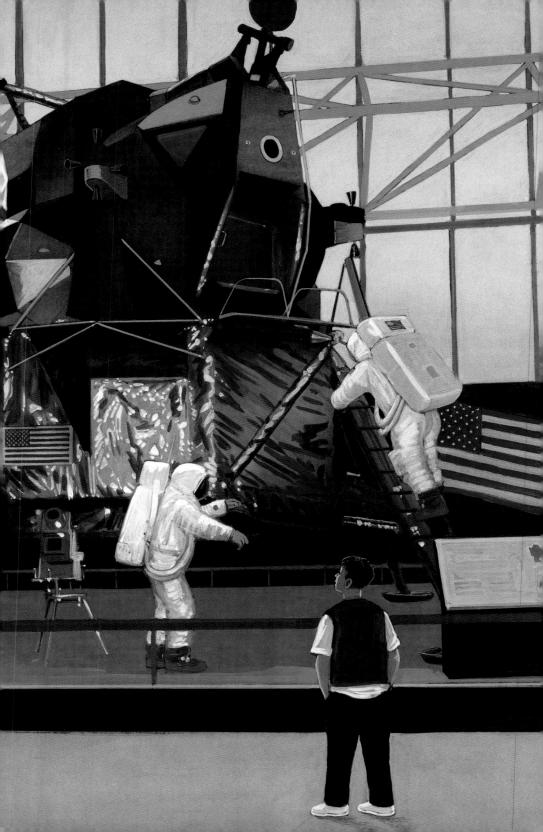

Chapter 2
Swimming in Space

Tomas feels like he is swimming. There is no **gravity**! And his clothes feel weird. He looks down to find he's wearing a space suit with the name NEIL ARMSTRONG stitched on the front. Two **astronauts** are with him. He knows them from his books in school. They are Buzz Aldrin and Mike Collins from the Apollo 11 mission!

"Mission Commander, are you ready?" Aldrin asks Tomas.

Tomas can't figure out how he got here. He once saw a movie where a boy was sent back in time. Could this be happening to him?

"Okay, I'll figure this out," Tomas whispers to himself as he looks around.

"There's Aldrin. There's Collins. And, here I am, wearing Neil Armstrong's space suit. We're on the Apollo 11. This is a famous day!"

Tomas looks toward the pointed end of the spacecraft *Columbia*, where the landing module *Eagle* is attached. If everything goes right, *Eagle* will soon begin its descent and in just a few hours, it will touch down on the moon. Tomas realizes that if he is really Neil Armstrong, he will soon be walking on the moon!

"Time to power up," says Aldrin, as he turns some dials.

"Um, excuse me, Mr. Aldrin," tries Tomas. "Sir? There's something you need to know. You see, I'm not really Neil Armstrong." But Tomas can't be heard over the radio.

He starts to panic. "Mr. Aldrin! Please! You have to listen to me. I'm not an astronaut. I'm just a kid!"

But nobody hears Tomas. He is buckled in next to Aldrin on *Eagle*. He looks back and sees the tiny planet Earth in the distance.

Chapter 3
Relax!

Tomas still can't believe what is happening to him. It's like a dream come true. Only now that it's real, Tomas is very scared. His heart pounds as *Eagle* backs away from *Columbia*. Tomas wishes he could stay with Collins in *Columbia*. He would be safe there, **orbiting** miles above the moon. But he is going down to the moon's surface and he needs to focus.

"Let's hope *Eagle* can really fly," says Tomas to himself. They head for their landing site on the moon.

"I can do this," Tomas whispers.
"The computer does all the work. I just
need to relax. I need to sit back and
enjoy the ride."

But Tomas' heart pounds wildly.
He breathes deeply. Just as he starts
to relax, numbers start flashing on the
computer display. Tomas radios Mission
Control that they have a program alarm.

"It's a 1202," Tomas reports to
Mission Control. His voice is shaky.
"What is it?" he asks Aldrin.

Chapter 4
Cloud of Dust

Aldrin realizes that a program alarm 1202 means the computer is overloaded. Tomas stares in fear as *Eagle* speeds toward a moon crater as big as a football field, filled with rocks as big as cars! Aldrin is busy checking the computer. He doesn't even notice the boulders!

Tomas knows that if the computer can't pilot *Eagle*, then the Mission Commander has to do it. Tomas thinks for a moment. Suddenly, he has a sinking feeling in his stomach.

If Tomas is Armstrong, *he* is Mission Commander!

Tomas knows that Armstrong is a good pilot. Armstrong has even flown in space before. Tomas hopes that he has Armstrong's abilities!

Tomas looks for a landing site. He steers left, but all he sees are rocks. Soon he spots a smooth surface. He sees it just in time! There is only enough fuel left for about 30 seconds of flight!

Suddenly, *Eagle's* engine kicks up a huge cloud of dust. Tomas can't see anything through the dust. He feels the ship going down very fast. He squeezes his eyes shut.

Then—*plop*. They land on the western edge of the **Sea of Tranquility**.

"That's it?" Tomas whispers. It doesn't feel like they've landed at all. Tomas slowly opens his eyes. A smile quickly spreads across his face. He did it! He landed *Eagle*! Tomas grabs the radio. He should let Mission Control know they are okay. Still shocked, Tomas picks up the radio.

"Houston, Tranquility Base here. The *Eagle* has landed."

Chapter 5

Bouncing on the Moon

According to the flight plan, Tomas and Aldrin are supposed to take a four-hour nap before leaving *Eagle*. In case they have to make an emergency lift off, they will be rested. But Tomas can't imagine sleeping now.

"I haven't taken a nap since I was three! I want to go now!" Tomas says.

Aldrin and Mission Control agree. After all, everyone is eager to see them walk on the moon.

Tomas and Aldrin have a lot to do before they leave the cabin. First they **depressurize** the cabin. Then they put on the three layers of their space suits. They strap on the heavy backpacks that hold their **life support systems**. Finally, they open the hatch.

Tomas gasps! *Eagle* is sitting on a wide, level plain, scattered with rocks and boulders—The Sea of Tranquility. The surface is chalky and gray. Tomas can't believe he is about to take his first step on the moon!

Tomas feels his heart begin to pound again as he switches on the camera mounted to the side of *Eagle*. When he does, 600 million people on Earth begin watching his every step on their televisions.

Backing down from *Eagle's* ladder, Tomas hops onto the landing pad. He carefully lifts his right boot and plants it on the moon's dusty surface. He bounces up and down like a rubber ball!

He begins to lift his other foot, but he quickly stops. "Oops, I should say Armstrong's famous words before I continue!" Tomas laughs to himself. Then he clears his throat and says, "That's one small step for man, one giant leap for mankind."

Tomas springs across the moon's surface, laughing at how strange it feels to hop along.

"I can jump so far! And I can jump in slow motion!"

Tomas continues springing across the moon like a kangaroo.

Soon Aldrin joins Tomas. It's time to start collecting moon rocks.

Tomas grabs his metal scoop and starts searching for samples. He feels like a pirate digging for lost treasure. He scoops up a pile of rocks, but most of them scatter away. He catches one rock in his glove and turns it around in his hand. It is small and light gray with a tiny chip in it. Inside the chip, it is almost black.

They collect rocks until their rock boxes are full.

Tomas and Aldrin set up lunar experiments for the scientists on Earth. Mission Control tells them they can stay on the moon's surface for fifteen more minutes. Tomas is disappointed he won't have more time on the moon.

He hops over to a giant crater, landing right at the edge of the pit. It looks like a huge empty swimming pool. As he starts to go over the edge to get to the bottom, Tomas comes to a halt!

Chapter 6

Moon to Museum

Tomas has a terrible thought. What if he gets stuck down there? Aldrin is too far away to save him. Instead of going down, Tomas uses his space camera to take pictures of the giant crater. He then returns to the landing site.

Tomas and Aldrin spend their last few minutes on the moon taking samples of the rocks around the base of *Eagle*. They have been outside on the moon's surface for nearly three hours. It is time for them to climb back up the ladder and take off.

As he climbs, Tomas looks over his shoulder for one last look at the moon. He doesn't want to leave—there is so much more to explore!

"Tomas, we can see the moon rock first if you want," Lucy says.

Tomas turns to her and looks around, confused. He's back at the museum! He looks down. He is wearing jeans and a t-shirt, not a space suit. He's a ten year old boy again.

"But, Lucy, you wouldn't believe where I just—" Tomas stops before finishing. Lucy would never believe he just came from the moon!

Tomas looks at Lucy with a smile. "Thanks, Lucy, let's go see that rock!"

Tomas runs ahead of the others. He can't wait to show his friends what a moon rock looks like. After all, he knows what it's like to hold one!

Glossary

Astronaut: a person trained to pilot or participate in the flight of a spacecraft.

Depressurize: to reduce the pressure inside a spacecraft to a similar level found outside, so astronauts can adapt to their new surroundings.

Gravity: the force that draws all bodies toward the center of a mass and gives them weight.

Life support system: an artificial or natural system that provides all or some of the items necessary for maintaining life or health.

Orbit: to revolve around an object.

Planetarium: a model or representation of the solar system and the night sky.

Sea of Tranquility: the landing site on the moon chosen for the Apollo 11 astronauts, due to its flat landscape.

About the First Moon Landing

In 1961, President John F. Kennedy challenged the American people to land a man on the moon before the end of the decade. In 1969, the Apollo 11 astronauts met the challenge. The flight of Apollo 11 was one of the most widely followed events in human history. About 600 million people watched at least part of the historic journey on television.

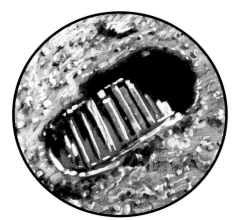

Neil Armstrong, Edwin "Buzz" Aldrin and Michael Collins began their journey on July 16, 1969. Four days later, the lunar module *Eagle* separated from the command module *Columbia* and began its descent. On July 20, 1969, Neil Armstrong and Buzz Aldrin became the first people ever to step onto the surface of the moon.

On the moon, the astronauts' main goal was to collect rocks and set up scientific experiments. But they also had time to take pictures and put up an American flag. Armstrong and Aldrin also left a plaque on the moon. It said: Here Men From Planet Earth First Set Foot Upon The Moon July 1969 A.D. We Came In Peace For All Mankind.

On July 24, 1969, the astronauts aboard *Columbia* splashed down in the Pacific Ocean. Once they were safely aboard the aircraft carrier USS *Hornet*, the astronauts were welcomed home by an excited nation!